The Monster on the Bottom Bunk

By
Geoffrey talboy

Illustrated By: MARY KERSHISNIK

DEDICATION

For Ben, Ollie, Tommy and Tony. Thank you for always inspiring me to have fun!

THERE'S A MONSTER ON MY
BOTTOM BUNK

HE SLEEPS THERE
EVERY NIGHT

I KNOW HE WAITS
FOR ME TO REST

AND GIVES ME
QUITE A FRIGHT

HIS GIANT BODY IS FULL OF
SCALES THAT BURST OUT
INTO FUR

HIS EYES ARE
BURNING RED

AND EACH FOOT HAS
A GIANT SPUR

HIS BREATH IS BURNING
FIRE, THAT SMELLS OF
OLD SARDINES

HE FILLS THE ROOM WITH
ALL THE GAS
MY WORD, IT'S QUITE
OBSCENE!

SHARP TALONS SPIKE OFF
EACH LARGE PAW
AND SCRATCH ME UNDER
MY MATTRESS

I WOULD YELL
AT HIM TO STOP
BUT I'M SURE
IT'D BE DISASTROUS

IN HIS MOUTH IS A SIX
FORKED TONGUE
AND TEETH IN SEVEN ROWS

A GIANT TAIL THAT
CURLS AROUND
AND WRAPS ALONG
HIS TOES

WHEN HE ROARS IT HURTS
MY EARS, I PULL THE
BLANKET CLOSE.

I'M SO AFRAID HE'S JUST
WAITING TO TURN ME
INTO TOAST!

THERE'S A MONSTER ON MY
TOP BUNK

HE SLEEPS THERE
EVERY NIGHT

I KNOW HE WAITS
FOR ME TO REST

AND GIVES ME
QUITE A FRIGHT

HIS SKIN IS BARE AND HE
ALWAYS SMELLS LIKE
SAUSAGE

HE MAKES A GROWUNG
COUGHING SOUND-
IF I WERE BRAVER,
I'D OFFER HIM A LOZENGE

HIS FINGERS NUMBER FIVE ACROSS
WITH LONG FLAT BLADES ON EACH

AND WHEN HIS TOES CLAW AT THE
WALL, IT MAKES A HIDEOUS SCREECH!

THE FUR ON HIS HEAD IS ALWAYS MAD.
IT SPIKES FROM EVERY PLACE

AND HE HAS TWO ORBS AND A LUMP
RIGHT IN THE MIDDLE OF HIS FACE!

WAIT!
YOU DOWN THERE, ARE YOU
REALLY AFRAID OF ME?!?

OF COURSE I AM! YOU'RE THE
MONSTER, THAT'S THE WAY IT
SHOULD BE!

NO I'M NOT, YOU ARE,

I CAN TELL YOU RIGHT AWAY!

IF YOU PLAN TO EAT ME, I'D

PREFER YOU GO AWAY

LOOK, I'M NOT A MONSTER, I'M JUST A LITTLE BOY.

I PROMISE I'M NOT SCARY!

WERE YOU AFRAID OF ME AS WELL?

IS IT BECAUSE I'M HAIRY?

OH NO, HOW SILLY! LOOK AT

US... WE WERE BOTH

AFRAID OF THE OTHER

BUT NOW I THINK WE'LL

BE QUICK FRIENDS WE'LL

PROTECT THIS BUNK

FOREVER!

I'M SO GLAD THAT WE ARE
FRIENDS THOUGH WE ARE SO
OPPOSITE. BUT WHAT DO WE
DO NOW, WITH THE MONSTER
IN THE CLOSET?

THE END